First U.S. edition 2011

Library of Congress Cataloging-in-Publication Data is available.
Library of Congress Catalog Card Number pending
ISBN 978-0-7636-5327-9

11 12 13 14 15 16 CCP 10 9 8 7 6 5 4 3 2

Printed in Shenzhen, Guangdong, China

This book was typeset in Lucy Cousins.
The illustrations were done in gouache.

Candlewick Press
99 Dover Street
Somerville, Massachusetts 02144

visit us at www.candlewick.com

Maisy Goes to the City

Lucy Cousins

CANDLEWICK PRESS

Today, Maisy and Charley are visiting their friend Dotty in the city.

Bus Station

Dotty is waiting for them at the bus station. "Welcome!" she calls.

The street outside the station is really busy.
BROOM, VROOM, BEEP!

What a lot of traffic, and what giant buildings!

The sidewalks are crowded, so Maisy, Charley, and Dotty have to walk slowly.

There are lots and
LOTS of shops.

"Come and see the toy store," Dotty says. "It's huge!"

When the walk signal flashes, it's safe to cross the street.

The store is full of shoppers!
Charley likes the escalators.
Maisy likes the elevators.

The toys are fabulous!
Charley wants to play
with them all.

Maisy sees one to give to Dotty
as a present.

She pays for it, but—
oh dear!—
where are
the others
now?

"Are you lost?"
Suddenly Maisy
wishes she was
safe at home.

Peacock makes
an announcement
on the intercom.

"There you are,
Maisy!" Dotty
holds her friend's
hand tight.

Then it's time to eat!
Dotty brings them
to a café in a square.

A guitarist plays music while the friends share a pizza.

Afterward, they play.
Even the park is busy in
the city!

To get to Dotty's apartment, they need to take a subway train.

"Our stop's on the blue line," Dotty says.

They squish into the subway car.

Hang on tight, everyone!

"Thank you," says Maisy.
"It's been a lovely day."

Outside, it's nearly dark.

The city lights
are bright and busy.

The stars are shining too.
They'll go twinkle,
twinkle, twinkle
all night long.